Acknowledg

This book would not have finally gone to
encouragement and editorial support f
detail, humour and wise suggestions have been invaluable.
Thanks also to Patrinia, whose unique artistic talent and design has made
the book come alive more than I could have hoped for as we worked
together on the layout and characters.
Finally to my loved ones, Poppy Grace, Lizzie and Gemma for proof reading
and making such helpful suggestions.

Thank you also to Ian Sherred for the final proof read and to
Callum at Hayling Print.

A donation of every book sold will be gifted to the Sustainability Centre.
The Centre sits in the heart of Hampshire's South Downs National Park.
This charity is a learning and residential centre for schools and adults and
show cases practical solutions to inspire and enable people to become the
planet protectors and change makers that our world needs.

WARNING

Please do not pick or eat any plants without being 100% sure of what they
are and what they can do. Follow the guidance of a plant specialist as
some are poisonous and some are legally protected. Never take more than
you need as they work together to help maintain our nature's balance.

1

Contents

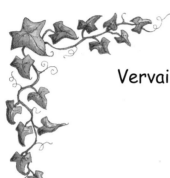

Chapter One
Vervain – The Enchanter's Plant

"If you don't let me know where you are going, I'll tell Mum!"

"If you must know, Bossy Boots, I'm going to see a Druid!" Sometimes Jack's sister, Ruby could be really annoying. And it was really none of her business.

"Why are you going to see a dude?"

Jack rolled his eyes. "Not a dude! A Druid. A Dru—id!"

"OK, OK. A Dru—id," mimicked Ruby. "Why are we going to see a Druid?"

"We? We? What makes you think you are coming?"

"I've never seen a Druid before."

"You don't even know what a Druid is," sneered Jack.

"I bet you don't, either."

"Yes I do!"

"Well, what is it?" persisted his sister.

Jack couldn't resist the opportunity to show off. "It's not an 'it'. A Druid is a person. Druids were the priests and teachers in ancient Celtic cultures. They were able to talk to the spirits of the plants and were treated with great respect."

Ruby was not impressed. "You just googled that," she smirked.

"So what if I did?"

"I still don't see why it's so important to go and see this Druid."

"Well, if you would listen for a bit I will try and explain." Jack surprised himself with his patience, but, after all, Ruby was two years younger than him.

"I had a dream the other night, or rather, I had a dream that keeps repeating itself. A wise old man dressed in white robes told me I had important work to do and that he would help me. He explained that he was a Druid Master and that I had to do my bit to heal the Earth."

"Didn't he tell you what you have to do?"

"More questions! He said that if I came to the woods to find him he would explain."

"So? What are we waiting for?"

"What makes you so sure you can come along too?"

"Oh!" She stopped and thought for a moment. "You know I like anything to do with helping our environment. Maybe two brains might be better than one?"

Jack knew she was right. She was his bright little sister who had masses of courage.

"Ok, so am I allowed to come with you?" asked Ruby, crossing her fingers behind her back.

"Only if you keep quiet, watch and listen and don't ask any stupid questions!"

"Great!" said Ruby. "Let's go!"

Jack smiled at her and shook his head.

"You can't come..." began Jack.

"You just said I could!" his sister interrupted.

"I was going to say, you can't come dressed like that." Jack now whispered as he moved towards the door, "You're still in your pyjamas!"

"Wait!" Ruby dashed to her room.

Soon they were quietly closing the back door behind them and running to the gate at the top of the garden.

"Here goes," exclaimed Jack, taking a deep breath. He was excited but a little apprehensive as to what they might find as they walked into the ancient wood.

It was a quiet, still evening in May. There was no sound in the ancient wood but every living creature was watching and listening. The only star shining in the heavens was the Dog Star – Sirius.

A tall, majestic figure walked through an opening in the trees. He was dressed in long white robes and wore a gold amulet on his chest. His long silver beard caught a glint of the star's magic light and his deep blue eyes followed the fireflies dancing around his head.

Everyone was watching the Druid Master.

He stooped in front of a plant - a fine, delicate structure with long purple flower spikes. He chanted over it and, drawing a circle in the Earth with his staff, he gently pulled the fragile plant from the ground. The Druid took care not to break its long stems and leaves and put an offering of fresh honeycomb on the earth in its place.

The Druid's eyes fixed on Jack's. He took the plant and gave it to him and began to chant an ancient song which stirred the memory of all who were listening.

"Oh sacred Vervain, our ancient herb. You who have the wisdom of the world. We honour you and thank you." His whole manner was very serious. Jack was thinking he wasn't someone you could have a joke with.

He then turned to Jack. "Use this Vervain to inspire you on your journey. It will give you clairvoyant powers. When you ask for guidance, it will show you the way."

"Excuse me Sir," Ruby spoke out now. "Why can't you go?"

"Shhh Ruby!"

"Good question young lady. It has to be young innocents like you two. You have been chosen because you can walk through the woods without being noticed - or so we hope."

"Where are we going anyhow?"

"You are going to search for a healing plant called Wood Betony, or the Elves' Cure. More will be revealed as you begin your journey."

As he spoke a hawk flew over their heads. "Let the hawk and nature spirits guide you in your quest. Too much information at this point might not be a good thing."

Ruby thought this was very odd but didn't like to ask any more questions.

Jack took the sacred plant and as he held it he felt calmness go through his whole body and a certainty that he was on the right path.

"This is what I have dreamed of doing," said Jack as he put the Vervain in his rucksack and turned to Ruby. Hand in hand they walked deeper into the wood.

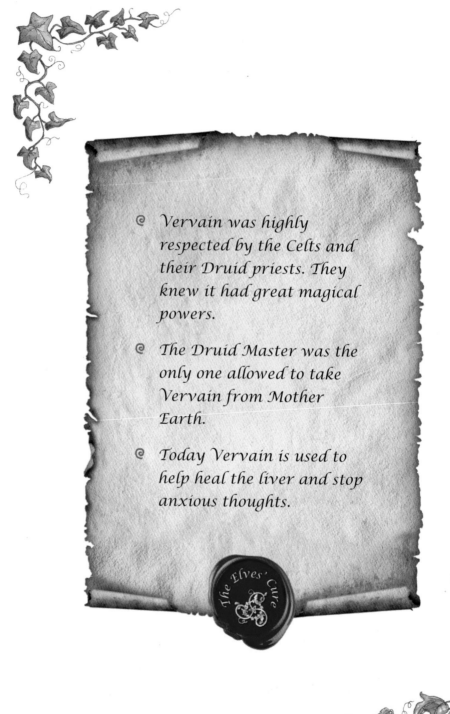

Vervain was highly respected by the Celts and their Druid priests. They knew it had great magical powers.

The Druid Master was the only one allowed to take Vervain from Mother Earth.

Today Vervain is used to help heal the liver and stop anxious thoughts.

Chapter Two

Wood Betony- The Healer of the Elf Sickness

Ruby (so called because of the colour of her hair) was pleased she'd dressed sensibly and put on her walking boots. She was shorter than her brother but what she lacked in size she certainly made up for in common sense. She smiled to herself as she looked at Jack's trainers.

"Daft boy", she thought.

Jack had his rucksack with secret pockets, a penknife, compass and a very precious plant.

The two young people walked deeper into the darkening wood following the only path they could find. Jack was aware of strange nature spirits all around them, guiding their footsteps. They were no taller than the bluebells at Jack's feet and their fine bodies seemed to shimmer with green and blue light. These were young elves and, as they danced around the young couple's ankles, Jack began to understand the words they were chanting.

"Stand still, Ruby. I can hear what these little creatures are saying. Can you?"

"I can't see or hear anything. What are you talking about?"

Jack had always known he had a special gift - that he could see nature spirits and hear their voices. It was only when he started school and his classmates teased him that he decided to stop talking about what he could see.

"Look carefully behind the bluebells. You will start to see tiny spirits. They are talking to us!" smiled Jack, happy that he could understand them.

"Be aware of the power of Betony."

"This is the plant we have to find," gasped Jack. "I know it! Shhh! There is more!" he whispered. Reluctantly, Ruby kept quiet.

"You must find it and bring it to cure the Elf Sickness. Betony will heal us and help reduce the conflict and hurt between the elven community and mankind."

"Mankind?" queried Jack. "What's mankind got to do with the Elf Sickness?"

"It is mankind who seems determined to destroy Mother Nature and us as well!"

Ruby was beginning to understand the elves chanting and felt that she had been silent long enough, so decided to be brave.

"Excuse me. Tell us about the Elf Sickness. What exactly is it?"

"Look all around you," said a young elf. "We dance and play but our elven elders can't do so any longer.

They sit dreaming under the old trees. They have lost their energy and magic."

"Why? What has happened?" asked Ruby.

"Selfishness and ignorance," said one elf, scratching his long hairy ears.

"Humans are destroying all of our sacred sites and places of healing where we go to restore our energy. The plants are dying too as the land changes. Our woods are no longer respected or cared for like they have been in the past. When trees were used by humans, they showed us true gratitude. They coppiced the hazel trees to encourage more growth, they used the dead wood for their fires and allowed the woodland to replenish. Now no-one does anything to maintain balance! Rubbish collects and pollutes the soil and trees are brutally torn down by young people who seem to know no better!"

Ruby was remembering her Forest School lessons. Her class had been taught how to care for the local woodland which benefitted all the creatures that lived in it. She had learned why it is important to protect the environment. This was all starting to make such a lot of sense, except for the elves!

The smallest elf was shedding a tear now. "The trees are hurting and crying in pain."

The two humans looked around them and yes, plastic bags and tin cans littered the pathways. Branches of trees had been broken off and some saplings torn from the ground. They both felt so ashamed of what humans had done.

Jack was the first to speak. "This doesn't look good."

"What can we do?" asked Ruby. "I don't see what we can do to help."

"Go find the magical Wood Betony and bring it to the elven elders," said a sad -looking elf. "We can plant it throughout the woodland again so that its energy, and that of the wood, will be restored."

"This sounds serious," thought Ruby. Jack was busy talking to the young elves but she couldn't catch what they were saying.

The elves gave the children fruits and honey-bee nectar and danced around them joyously singing and playing. For a brief moment, they forgot their worries.

An older, more serious elf came up to them and sat quietly watching them eat.

"I have something to show you. Follow me." He led them to a pool of spring water a short distance away. "Eat some of your sacred Vervain. Yes, we know you have been given it and then look into the water. You will be shown the next part of your journey."

Filled with curiosity, Ruby and Jack did as the elf had instructed. They were still shocked by what the elves had told them and wanted to do something to help.

The clear water changed in shape and an image of a beautiful ancient tree appeared. Its roots were curling into a brook which bubbled gently over them.

Jack felt himself shaking with fear, but he glanced quickly at Ruby. She was staring with curiosity at the image. She was stunned into silence which was unheard of but her lack of fear gave Jack courage.

"Find this place and the spirit will be there to greet you. Oh, and take this flask of spring water too. You will need it."

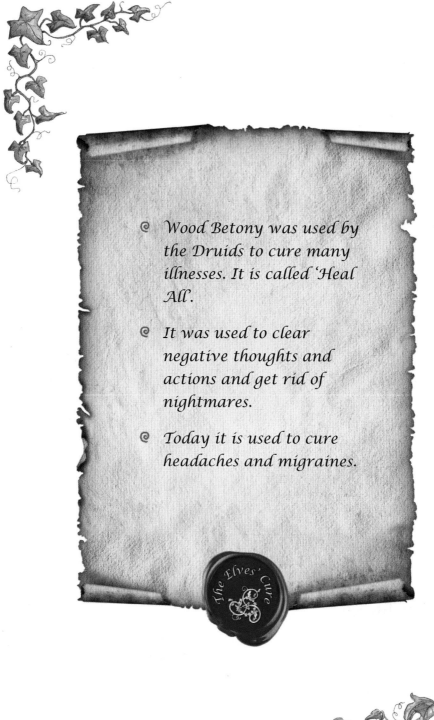

@ Wood Betony was used by the Druids to cure many illnesses. It is called 'Heal All'.

@ It was used to clear negative thoughts and actions and get rid of nightmares.

@ Today it is used to cure headaches and migraines.

The Elves' Cure

Chapter Three
Aqua & Burdock

So it was that the young pair began their journey –
taking the flask of fresh spring water and Vervain
with them.

They moved slowly through the thickening brambles.
Jack turned his head in time to see the brambles
closing the path behind them. He didn't want to
frighten Ruby by telling her, but he was aware that
his heart was beating faster and there were some
beads of perspiration on his forehead. Over their
heads, a hawk was circling and Jack hoped it was
there to help them. Jack took out his compass but
the arrows kept spinning round and round.

A screeching sound was becoming louder. Although
it seemed familiar, he couldn't quite work out what
the sounds were until he remembered what the

Druid had told them. "You need to follow the hawk wherever it takes you."

It was then that they stumbled across a rippling stream.

"I think this is the water we have to follow," said Ruby and she marched off, headstrong as always. They clambered over rocks and slipped into rock pools until eventually they came to a curve in the stream where the only crossing point in the deeper water was by the roots of an old tree.

"I'm sure this is it," said Ruby as she sat on one of the heavy roots, exhausted from their trek. She took off her boots and let the cold water caress her aching feet. Jack was still trying to get his compass to work.

Suddenly, she was aware of a movement in the water - the shining reflection was more than hers. In fact, it was a beautiful face smiling back at her through the silvery water. She started backwards with a shriek and nearly fell into the stream, but Jack was there to catch her.

"What have you seen? What's the matter?"

"I wish I knew," she answered. "It was a face shining and smiling out through the water at me. It seemed to be made of sparkling crystals, the size of teardrops." They looked together into the water but the face had gone.

"How disappointing," Jack sighed out loud. He was getting used to magical happenings and had a feeling this one was quite safe.

"Let's wait. I'm sure they will come back," he said hopefully, but noting the disappointment in Ruby's face.

Sure enough, as they relaxed watching the rhythm of the water the face appeared again, still smiling. In a flash the body of a small fairy jumped out of the water and landed on the root beside them. She was indeed very sparkly and the tiny crystals over her fine body and wings glinted every time she moved.

"Good day to you. I'm Aqua, a sprite and the spirit protector of this stream."

"You made us jump!!" cried Jack.

"Well I suppose it's not every day you see a water spirit is it? Where was I? Oh yes. It's my job to protect this stream on its way to the big river. Not an easy job these days because of all the rubbish clogging up the flow. Then when it rains, the water starts to foam from something the farmer is putting on his fields. It kills the fish too. Not good news I'm afraid. All of my water spirit friends are the same, all struggling to keep our water clean."

Jack noted that she seemed quite cheerful considering she was carrying such bad news.

"What we need is a good dose of Burdock," continued Aqua. "If you find any on your travels please bring it back so we can grow it by the streams. It will help to keep them clean. It will keep you clean too!!"

"What does it look like?" asked Ruby. She was back in questioning mode. "I wish I had brought my iPad with me!"

"Who needs an iPad? We've got the Vervain to show us". Jack didn't mean to sound impatient with Ruby but she never stopped asking questions.

"Clever boy, but use it sparingly. I have a strong feeling you will need it several times on your quest." Aqua was serious now.

Jack ate a small leaf and again looked at the stream. The image of a familiar plant appeared.

"Yes! I recognise it! We used to call it 'Beggars Buttons' and threw the seeds at each other. It has huge leaves and when you look at the underside they are silvery grey. The seed heads are like balls of Velcro."

"It used to grow all around here too," said Aqua "but .... well, you know what I'm going to say."

"Yes," they both echoed. "Because of man's thoughtlessness in destroying the woods and polluting the water, it is no longer here," continued Ruby.

"When you come across the silver stream that hasn't been spoiled and holds great magic you will find the Burdock."

Jack was beginning to look concerned. "OK, OK. We already have to get Wood Betony for the elves and now Burdock!"

"That's great news!" cried Aqua. "Don't you see? Where you find one, you will find the other."

"You make it sound so easy!" sighed Jack, who was beginning to feel very weary.

"It won't be!" she smiled. "Now get a move on before it gets too dark to see your way to the river. Follow this stream and when you get to the river bank, rest and use your magic Vervain again. God speed dear ones."

"All too much for one day!" exclaimed Ruby. Jack agreed but he wasn't going to let his little sister think she was right.

"We seem to have been in the woods for ages but it is as if time has stood still."

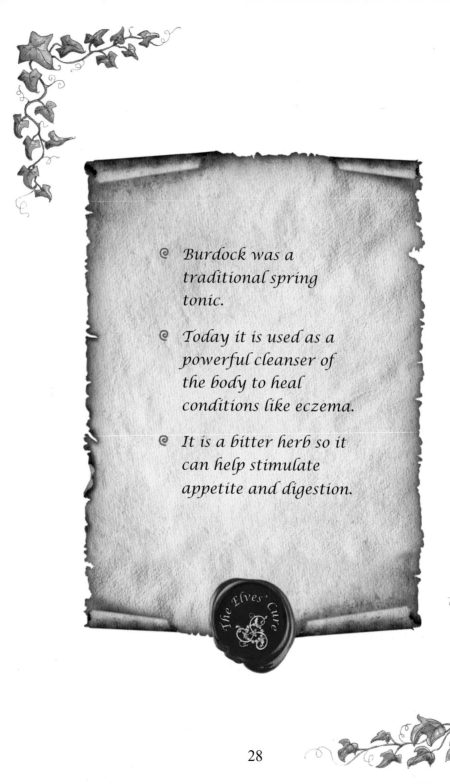

Burdock was a traditional spring tonic.

Today it is used as a powerful cleanser of the body to heal conditions like eczema.

It is a bitter herb so it can help stimulate appetite and digestion.

The Elves' Cure

Chapter Four

Oak – The Great Protector

Jack and Ruby moved on slowly and deeper into the wood. As they followed the stream, the shadows grew. At dusk, the trees and plants began to whisper to the young people.

Jack felt a tight knot in his stomach from trying hard to show that he was not scared. He thought that the path they had chosen kept changing in shape and direction. It seemed as if the brambles were moving, becoming larger and slightly sinister.

The whispering sound was like a sad lament. "Save us. Save us!" was all he could understand. Jack wished he had taken more notice of his dreams. He felt sure that he would have been given more guidance.

In time, exhaustion got the better of them and they rested by the trunk of an old oak tree. The roots were filled with rabbit holes and moss covered the ancient bark.

"This seems like a safe enough place to rest," said Jack, as he sat on the largest root he could find. They quietly ate the fruit the elves had given them and drank from the flagon of spring water. Ruby was the first to speak.

"I can feel a warm glow flowing through my whole body. Can you?"

Jack was too tired to answer her. He had curled up on the grass and, looking up, he saw the hawk circling above their heads. He knew it was protecting them – or so he hoped.

That night, both Ruby and Jack had wild dreams. They found themselves battling against dark spirits, crossing seas with bottomless depths and clinging to cliffs and perilous crevices. Yet, as they tossed and turned in their nightmare world, a green mist started to flow from the base of the tree, inching its way towards Jack and Ruby. As it expanded and darkened, it was clear it was alive, like a serpent and it sensed their presence. Closer and closer it came until it completely surrounded them. Ruby moaned in her sleep but didn't wake up. Neither she nor Jack was aware of what was going on. Not even when the shapeless mass slowly reached out to touch Jack!

Suddenly, the hawk screeched loudly and both Jack and Ruby woke with a start.

"Help! Help!" screamed Ruby. Jack turned just in time to see the mysterious green shape begin to change. "That, whatever-it-is," she cried, pointing a nervous finger at the mist, "was covering your rucksack, Jack!" I saw it in my nightmare but I couldn't move or call out. I was completely paralysed! Oh Jack, I'm so frightened." Ruby's face had turned white and she was visibly shaking.

Jack reminded himself of how young his brave little sister was and hugged her tightly.

"I know! It was pretty scary," said Jack, "but we seem to be safe now. Look! The green thing has changed into the shape of a huge oak leaf!"

Ruby was about to answer when another voice joined them.

"OK you two, time to get moving!" Standing in front of them was a gnome-like creature. It was a bit like the ones in their grandparents' garden, thought Jack, except this one had an extremely long grey beard that touched the ground and was rather thin. "This old oak has, in fact, given you rest and protection from the evil forces of your nightmares. That green cloak that wrapped itself around you was the spirit of the oak. But now it's time to gather up your strength for the hard journey ahead of you."

"Cool! Who, or what are you?" exclaimed Jack.

"Enough to say you stopped me getting a good night's sleep!"

"What do you mean?"

"You fell asleep at the entrance to my home, deep in the roots there. Can you see it? I didn't like to wake you so I slept outside. Not used to that I must say, and I could murder a cup of tea and some buttered toast."

"Umm, that would be rather nice," mused Ruby.

"OK. OK. I get the hint. Wait a bit and I will see what I can rustle up. Then you must hurry on your way. This wood is no longer a safe place for humans."

As they waited, they became aware of how hungry they were. The gnome returned with something hot that smelled like honey and a tiny offering of buttered toast no bigger than Ruby's finger, but as they ate it, they felt their stomachs getting full and very satisfied.

"Yummy," said Jack. "What was that?"

"It was just a touch of gnome magic, young man, which should stop you feeling hungry today. Now drink up and be on your way."

"Thank you for your kindness, Mr....?" questioned Ruby, who had impeccable manners.

"Call me... er... Georgius. Oh, and when you get to the underground cavern, please don't tell anyone there you have seen me."

The children didn't ask Georgius why. They were too concerned about the underground cavern. Surely nothing could be worse than being in a dark, ancient and increasingly sinister wood. Or so they thought! Jack could see the worried look on his young sister's face. Her nightmares had really frightened her.

Georgius watched the nervous siblings as they set off again down the path.

"Thank you for your help!" Ruby shouted back. Soon they were out of sight.

"Don't mention it," sniggered Georgius. "It was my pleasure!" And a wicked grin spread over his face.

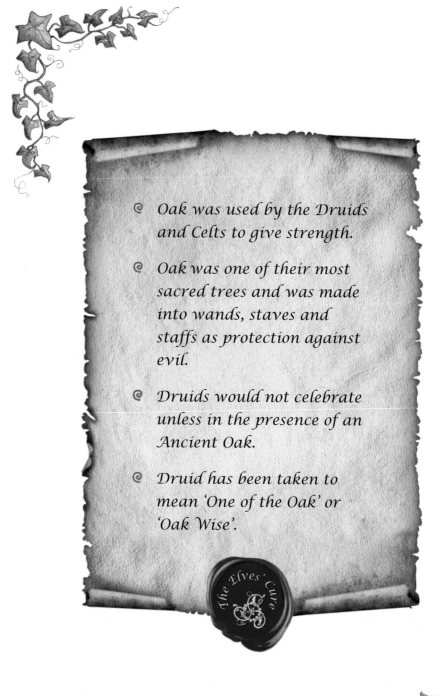

- Oak was used by the Druids and Celts to give strength.

- Oak was one of their most sacred trees and was made into wands, staves and staffs as protection against evil.

- Druids would not celebrate unless in the presence of an Ancient Oak.

- Druid has been taken to mean 'One of the Oak' or 'Oak Wise'.

The Elves' Cure

Chapter Five

The Ramson Maiden

The sun shone through the canopy of leaves onto a carpet of what looked like six-pointed stars. They were delicate white flowers, shining in the sunlight.

"Hey, this is cool. This smells of garlic!" said Jack, as he picked a few leaves at his feet. "I know that garlic is meant to ward off evil. I've seen it in old movies. I wonder if this will do the same thing."

Ruby began to pick a handful, walking gently across them so she didn't crush too many as she went. "They're so lovely! It's hard to believe this forest is so dangerous. Look at how bright green the leaves are."

"I think we may have a problem, Sis," interrupted Jack, staring up ahead. "There's a fork in the path. We need to decide, left or right."

"Let's use the Vervain and see what it tells us," suggested Ruby, keen to help but actually still feeling very scared. She hadn't recovered from her bad dreams and something about Georgius the Gnome bothered her, although she couldn't put her finger on it.

"OK, but just a little. We've been told not to use it all." Ruby cupped her hands. Jack poured a little of the precious spring water into them but before he had a chance to take out the Vervain, a beautiful white maiden rose up in front of them. She grew and grew until she was almost as tall as the young trees around her. The young couple had to strain their necks to see her face. She looked down, smiling. Jack and Ruby stood open-mouthed, not sure whether to stay or run away.

"Cool!" exclaimed Jack. This was definitely becoming his favourite word.

Ruby was more polite. Summoning up all her courage, she asked, "May I know your name?"

"I am the Spirit of the Ramsons. Yes, that is the name of this plant. You have nothing to fear from me. In fact, by taking my leaves you are protected from all evil ... well, at least for the time being."

"Thought so," interrupted Jack.

"If you will let me finish young man, there are dark forces that you will meet on your journey. These Ramsons will help to protect you by giving you courage as you face your worst fears. Go search for Mother Elder. She will also give you the strength you will need. This is not the time to be timid or faint-hearted, but then, that is why you have been chosen. Use the Ramsons wisely and remember to call on me for help. Oh, yes. I almost forgot! Take the *left* path!"

With that, she disappeared.

"What a shame," said Ruby. "I would like to have asked her more questions, like 'what are these dark forces?' and 'what do they want?' and 'what was that about Mother Elder?' We have an elder bush in our garden. Do you think she was talking about that?"

"Could be, I suppose," Jack frowned. "I didn't expect us to have to search for something else! And I didn't like what she said about dark forces."

"You didn't expect this to be easy, did you?" questioned Ruby. "Where there is good magic, there is always bad. That's the unwritten law. But we can choose which one to focus on. We just have to make sure the good magic is there all around us if we are to succeed. It says so in all my story books."

These were wise words for someone so young. Yet they both knew they made sense. There was no arguing about it. They just had to go where the Vervain took them.

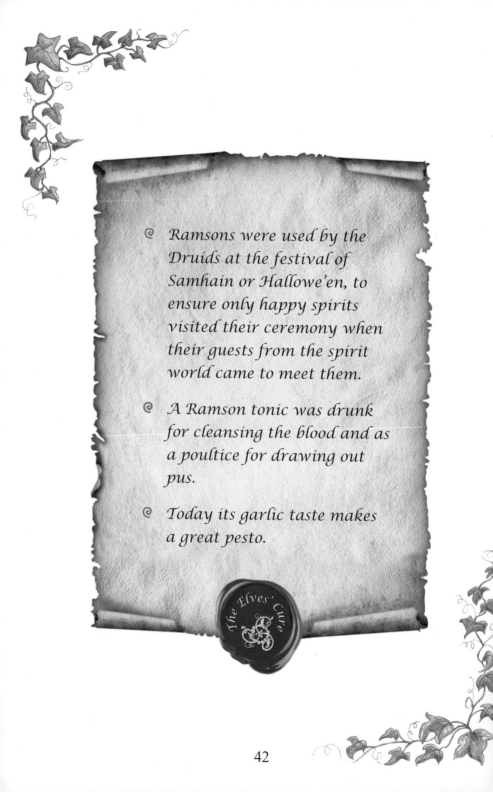

Ramsons were used by the Druids at the festival of Samhain or Hallowe'en, to ensure only happy spirits visited their ceremony when their guests from the spirit world came to meet them.

A Ramson tonic was drunk for cleansing the blood and as a poultice for drawing out pus.

Today its garlic taste makes a great pesto.

Chapter Six

The Search for Mother Elder

Ruby and Jack took the left-hand path as the Ramson Maiden had suggested and walked to the very edge of the ancient forest. Then, they came out into bright daylight. For whatever reason, they chose to keep to the edge of the field and only saw the occasional insect. In the past, the fields would have been swarming with them and there would have been bees and butterflies everywhere amongst the wild flowers. Yet, even the hayfields had only a scattering of poppies and chamomile flowers.

Jack looked puzzled. "I know what we are looking for. A tree laden with creamy blossoms and smelling like sweet honey. But this isn't right."

"The hedgerows have all been gashed bare and the only tree we have seen had few leaves and looked very sad. And where are the birds?" added Ruby.

They walked on, quite saddened and were pleased to leave the fields behind them. At this point they had no idea where they were going. There was still no sign of an elder tree.

"This is a bit of a mystery," said Jack. "I know that the Elder is a sacred tree so perhaps we will find it by a sacred site!"

Ruby asked the obvious question. "What does a sacred site look like?"

"Who knows? I think we'll only find the answer to that question when we find a site!"

Eventually, the children came to a tiny stream. They both knew that following it would lead them back into the ancient wood which neither was very keen on doing. But it looked as if there was no choice. Each took a deep breath and Jack and Ruby followed the stream back into the shadows. This time, they quickly noticed that the water seemed to flow underground.

"Odd!" said Jack. "Guess we've lost it now."

"Wait a minute. Listen! I can hear a gentle trickling sound. Look! Over there!" exclaimed his sister, quite pleased with her discovery.

Sure enough, the water was pouring out into a small well. Ivy had woven its way around what looked like an ancient inscription carved into a stone.

"That's no help!" complained Ruby. "It's in a strange language. I can't even make out the letters."

"Now is the time to use the Vervain!" replied Jack excitedly, as he rummaged in his rucksack. After searching for a moment or two, Jack stood up and emptied the contents of his rucksack onto the ground. "I can't understand it!" he moaned. "The Vervain has gone!"

Ruby pushed Jack out of the way. "Let me look! It can't have gone!" On her hands and knees, she searched through all the items lying on the ground.

But her brother wasn't mistaken. There was no Vervain to be seen. "Are you sure you put it back after the last time we used it?" She could hear the despair in her own voice.

Jack was hesitant. "We were going to use it when we were with the Ramson Maiden, but we didn't need to. So, the last time we used it … "

"I know!" cried Ruby. "It was before we fell asleep under the oak tree, before we met the gnome. We've not spoken to anyone else."

Ruby thought for a moment. Suddenly, it all made sense. "Georgius must have taken it when we were asleep!" she shouted. "I didn't trust him at the time, I didn't know why but I do now!" Poor Ruby was feeling very miserable. "We'll just have to go and get our Vervain back from that thieving gnome!"

Ruby had actually started to head back along the path but stopped when she realised that her brother wasn't following her. Jack hadn't moved. Then, looking at Ruby, he started to smile.

"What are you smiling for?" she asked.

"It's OK, Ruby. I've just remembered! I've got some Vervain in my rucksack's secret pockets. I put it there for safe keeping!"

"Clever you! I'm so proud of my big brother."

"Don't overdo it! Just a bit of luck really." But Jack knew he had listened to his inner voice and that guidance was often there when he paid attention.

"Now it *is* time to take the Vervain!"

He gave Ruby a piece of their precious plant to eat with a sip of water from the well. Slowly the inscription on the stone became clearer and Ruby read the words aloud:

> "Blessed be this sacred site and the water that pours forth.
>
> Blessed be Mother Earth that lives on this water.
>
> Blessed be the sacred Elder that it feeds."

Ruby noticed something. "There is a tree here Jack, but it hasn't any flowers."

"Try giving it some water," Jack suggested.

Together they carefully scooped up some water and took it to the tree.

"Wow! What magic was that!" exclaimed Jack. As the water had touched the tree, the buds burst into flowers. Yes, it was the magical Elder tree. The creamy blossoms smelled of honey and made them feel quite dizzy.

"Well, we've found the Elder tree but I don't see how that helps us." sighed Jack.

"I think we should say something, don't you?" Ruby was thinking hard now.

"Like what?" asked Jack, a little impatiently. "How can that help?"

"Don't be grumpy, Jack. Why don't we repeat the words we have just read and see what happens?"

They were both aware that they were losing patience with each other but didn't know why. Together they repeated the words and slowly more flowers began to appear on the tree. At the same time however, the children heard a gentle whispering voice reply from deep within its leaves:

"Good morning, young people. We have been waiting for you. The hedgerows are sad and the spirits are leaving. Your quest for the Betony has only just begun and you will have to be strong and brave. I am the guardian of this sacred well and I offer you some of my flowers to take with you as protection from dark forces and the dreaded Mondrilla, who is evil. Yes, I'm afraid your journey has been straightforward up to now. There are challenges ahead, but if you stay true to your quest and listen to the spirits of nature, that is all anyone can expect of you. Remember, always stay together. That is your greatest strength. Don't be tempted to walk separate paths. That leads to disaster."

They quietly took some elderflower blossoms and put them carefully into Jack's rucksack. Jack and his sister were silent, feeling that words would spoil the magic and also because, if they admitted it, both were a little frightened of Mother Elder and her power. Together, the children bowed low in front of the magic tree and quietly stepped backwards.

It was a good five minutes before either of them spoke. "We've already been told about the dark forces," said Jack, quietly, as they walked along, "but now the Evil One, Mondrilla! It doesn't sound very inviting, does it?"

Ruby didn't want to think about what her brother had just said. Both of them stared directly ahead, hoping whatever danger was there could be safely avoided. Perhaps that was why neither of them saw the misshapen creatures with the green eyes that were behind them... and slowly getting closer.

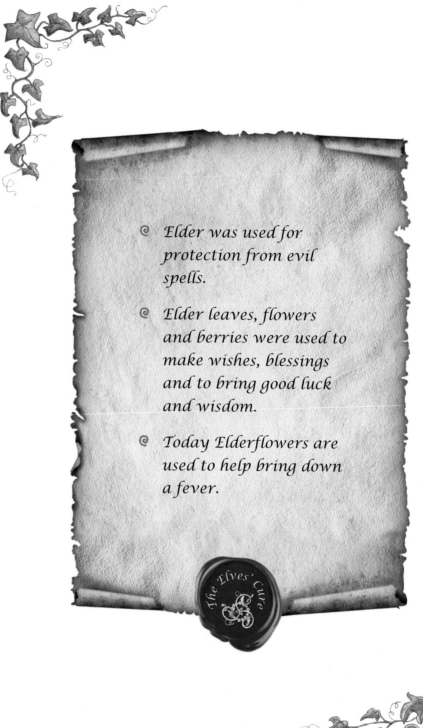

Elder was used for protection from evil spells.

Elder leaves, flowers and berries were used to make wishes, blessings and to bring good luck and wisdom.

Today Elderflowers are used to help bring down a fever.

The Elves' Cure

Chapter Seven

The Dragon on the Path

Ruby and Jack had seen the water spirit Aqua, had slept under an old oak and breakfasted with Georgius the gnome, who wasn't quite what he seemed. They had also met the White Maiden of the Ramsons and gone in search of Mother Elder, only to be given more bad news.

They had heard several times of dark forces in the wood and had now been warned to stay close because of Mondrilla. Silently, they both thought of what had already happened to them. It seemed that not only were they getting deeper into the woods, but deeper into trouble!

"I really don't like this," whispered Ruby, her voice quivering. As they continued walking, the path seemed to clear in front of them, although they couldn't see where it was going. In fact, everything around them seemed darker and the shadows made mysterious shapes.

"Keep to the path, Ruby. In fact, you had better hold my hand." Jack wasn't sure whether he was doing this for Ruby or himself but as he uttered the words they both became suddenly aware that the brambles were closing in around them. Jack glanced back and saw that the path behind them was already overgrown. He caught a glimpse of what looked like a pair of green eyes and held Ruby's hand even tighter.

"No going back now," he thought.

Suddenly, Jack felt his hand being squeezed really hard. He was about to ask Ruby what was the matter when he saw for himself what had frightened her. The path in front of them was moving from side to side like a slithering serpent. The children stood still. "Dark forces!" muttered Jack. What could they do? The path behind them was choked with brambles so there was no escape that way. They would both have to start walking along the bewitched path and hope for the best.

The wood suddenly became darker and darker yet at the same time their path, though still moving in its sinister way, was clear. It was as if the Elderflower in Jack's rucksack and the Ramsons in Ruby's hand were keeping away something that was most unpleasant!

Both youngsters were now aware of several pairs of bright green eyes watching them as they stood undecided what to do, but neither wanted to frighten the other.

"Oh, Jack!" exclaimed Ruby. "I really don't like this."

"Nor me. I guess we have to keep walking and just see what happens."

As he spoke these words, there was an almighty roar above their heads. They started to run but the roaring got louder and louder and the eyes looking at them brighter and more numerous.

"STOP!" They froze but were too frightened to turn around.

"NOW, BE STILL FOR A MOMENT, PLEASE!"

They couldn't believe their eyes. Landing on the path in front of them was a dragon with beautiful purple and green scales along its body and wings.

"AT LAST! NOW WATCH!"

With these words, the dragon opened its vast jaws and sent orange, scarlet and violet flames into the woodland. Nothing burned, but my goodness, there was a shrieking and yelping and hundreds of eyes instantly disappeared.

"THAT'S BETTER!" shouted the dragon. "NOW WE CAN WALK SAFELY."

"Why are you shouting at us?" asked Ruby, summoning up her courage.

"OH SORRY, BUT MY ROARING HAS MADE ME A BIT DEAF!"

"What happened to all the eyes?" Jack asked.

"THOSE EYES, YOUNG MAN, WERE MALICIOUS SPIRITS SENT BY MONDRILLA'S SPELL TO STOP YOUR JOURNEY."

"Sshh! Try whispering, can't you?" Complained Ruby covering her ears.

"OK," said the dragon, trying to be quiet. "I sent them scurrying away but they will come back in a while. So, I suggest that rather than talking, you run along and when the path climbs upwards you should be safe – for a while."

"Thank you, Mr Dragon," said Ruby, polite as always. "What do we call you?"

"My name is Dragus, Dragus the 30th. I come from 30 generations of dragonhood. My great, great, great, great, great, great grandmother wasn't very creative with names! So we got stuck with this!"

"But how do we know what path to follow? It keeps changing shape. And now it's dividing!" exclaimed Jack.

"I know. I know. It's Mondrilla's power. It uses its energy to change the shape of plants, paths, in fact, anything."

"So it's a shape shifter," noted Jack.

"Yes, so be very careful. Not everything will be what it seems!"

"Well, that explains Georgius!" exclaimed Ruby.

"Now, I must be going," said Dragus. "Goodbye now. We shall meet again near the end of your quest I am sure." And, with a swish of his purple green tail, he flew up into the trees and all was dark again.

"Oh heck, Mondrilla is a shape-shifter! I don't like this one bit," admitted Jack. "It's not only getting complicated, it's getting nasty!"

"Don't think, just walk!" said Ruby, firmly, as if to talk would get them into more trouble.

As they did so, the bushes and branches began to close in again.

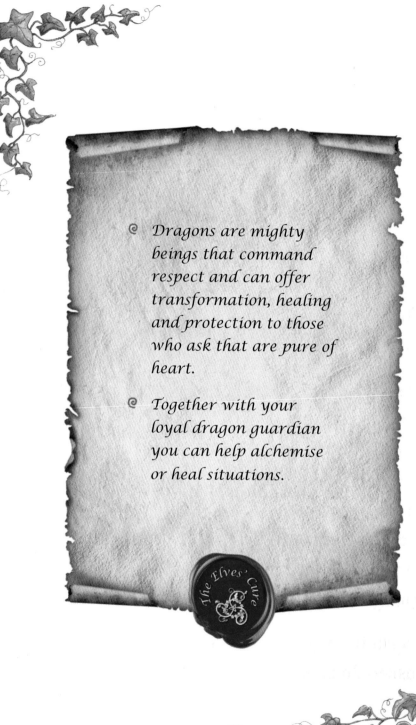

Dragons are mighty beings that command respect and can offer transformation, healing and protection to those who ask that are pure of heart.

Together with your loyal dragon guardian you can help alchemise or heal situations.

The Elves' Cure

Chapter Eight

The Magic Steps

Brother and sister walked on, nervously glancing behind from time to time, aware that the green eyes were back watching their every move, though this time at a distance.

After some time, they came to steps which were mysteriously carved out of the earth. The steps were covered in green moss and silvery ferns which shone as the children climbed them. It was almost as if the steps were alive. They seemed to go upwards in a circular fashion but once Jack and Ruby got to the final step, they found themselves at the bottom again!

"We seem to be getting nowhere fast! What's going on?" asked Jack, not expecting an answer.

"It's bit like a circular escalator. The steps are now moving as well!" observed Ruby. "And wherever we are trying to get to, someone or something doesn't want us to get there!"

"Ummm, evil malicious spells," mused Jack. "Why don't we try jumping two or three steps at a time and see if we can break the pattern ... if there is one?"

"Maybe it's time to use the Elderflower? It's meant to bring us good luck and keep us strong," suggested Ruby.

"OK, but we may have to jump at some point because these steps are moving faster and faster!"

The 'some point' was right in front of them and it looked like a huge black hole. "So much for being safe on the steps," commented Jack, in his usual slightly cynical way. "I guess we have two choices – keep speeding up on the steps and fall into that black ... thing! Or make a jump for it."

Before they had a chance to decide, the steps sped up so much that the pair began to lose their balance.

"Make a jump for it now or we might end up at the beginning again. And I sense there is something waiting there for us!"

"Yes, there's a dark shape moving up the steps!" cried Ruby, her anxiety clear in her voice.

"And those green-eyed things can't be far behind!" added Jack.

They had no idea what they were jumping into but something assured them that their herbs were looking after them. They did have the Elderflower in Jack's rucksack and Ruby was still holding the Ramsons, if a little too tightly now. Hoping the plants would protect them, they leapt into the darkness.

BUMP! They seemed to make a fairly soft landing.

"You OK?" asked Jack, as he heard Ruby give a low yelp of pain.

"I think so but I landed on my wrist."

"I'd have a look at it but I can't see a thing in this darkness! Do you think we are on even ground here?"

"I certainly hope so. Shhh! What was that rustling sound?"

They both fell silent, listening carefully.

"I can't hear anything," whispered Jack.

"There it is again!"

This time, Jack was aware of a sort of shuffling and snorting. And it was getting closer. Neither of the children could see anything in the inky darkness, but now it was so close they could hear it breathe.

"My goodness, you took some finding!" said a gruff voice.

Ruby and Jack peered into the darkness. Without realising it, they were holding on to each other very tightly.

"It's OK. I'm quite harmless. It's the others you need to watch out for! Only joking, my name is Tobin."

The creature lit a flaming torch. "That's better." But to be honest, Jack and his sister weren't sure.

They could make out a very round creature with strange pointed teeth. He wasn't a pretty sight but he seemed friendly enough.

"I know you will have loads of questions and there will be time for them later. But for now, follow me. The Green Eyes are getting a little too close for my liking."

They trod slowly and carefully down a winding staircase, aware that at the side there was nothingness. "Be careful. If you slip off the side, I can't save you."

Ruby held tightly onto Jack's hand, admitting to herself that she was really scared of heights and that it was better to hold on to someone who was stronger than her.

Eventually, the ground flattened out and they saw in front of them a silvery stream. "I'm sure that's the stream we were told about," whispered Ruby. "It looks like shiny liquid metal."

"Like mercury," said Jack, remembering his science lessons and beginning to wish he was back doing something quite normal.

Their companion held up his hand. "Wait here a minute. We have to ask the water's permission to cross and, because you are humans, it may not be very happy about that."

"I guess that's because of all the pollution we humans have created," whispered Ruby.

The Troll-like creature uttered words that neither Jack nor Ruby could understand. The silvery water stopped flowing.

"OK. Time to jump! Do exactly as I do and you will be fine." He took a huge leap, landed half way into the water and then leapt again to the other side.

"Here goes," said Jack, bravely, taking Ruby's good arm, but not sure why he trusted this creature, who could turn out to be yet another enemy - like Georgius! Together they followed in his footsteps, or rather, leaping steps. As they did so they were aware that the water seemed to come alive. It began to wrap itself around their legs and they found themselves being pulled down below its surface. With all their remaining energy, they took a huge leap to the other side.

"Phew. I'm glad that's over," exclaimed Jack, but Ruby was in too much pain to answer him.

"Here, take this." The Troll gave her a drink which was both pink and golden. "It is Poppy and Chamomile. It will calm you and help to take the pain away until I can look at your arm. It will also help you sleep."

That was something both the children definitely needed.

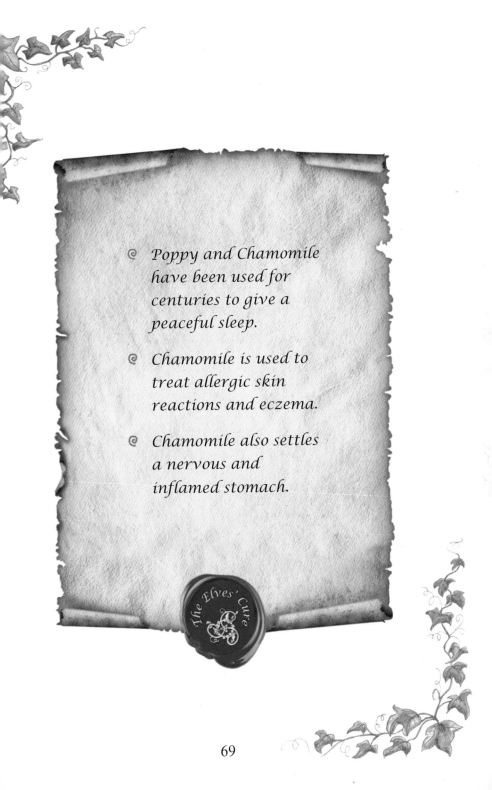

@ Poppy and Chamomile
   have been used for
   centuries to give a
   peaceful sleep.

@ Chamomile is used to
   treat allergic skin
   reactions and eczema.

@ Chamomile also settles
   a nervous and
   inflamed stomach.

The Elves' Cure

Chapter Nine

The Trolls' Story

Jack and Ruby awoke to the sound of gentle singing. The trolls were chanting an ancient song by the side of the silver stream. When they caught sight of the youngsters, they stopped and stared.

"You two look better," said Tobin. "Come and join us. We are singing to the stream so that it stays pure and magical."

Jack's stomach was rumbling and he couldn't remember when he had last eaten, though he wasn't sure he would want to eat anything the trolls gave him. As if reading his thoughts, Tobin came over to them.

"Time for some food - come with me." He led them to a small table laden with appetizing foods. They couldn't believe their eyes. "Will this be OK?" asked Tobin.

"Sure will!" they both replied. In front of them were wild strawberries and raspberries, plums, warm honey, lavender cakes and golden buttered scones.

"Now, before you start, we need to thank The River and Mother Earth for this food. Then, while you eat, I am going to tell you all about us."

Ruby and Jack were happy to wait. The food smelled so delicious - warm breads, perfumed honey, and fruit of all shapes and sizes. Soon they were happily eating and Tobin began.

"Our work is very important to Mother Earth. We clean the rivers and the roots of trees, getting the soil ready for growing. Sadly, the earth is becoming very polluted and smelly. It is very hard work cleaning it all. In fact, it's making us pretty smelly too!"

"Thought so," whispered Ruby to Jack.

"We used to work with humans. They accepted the Spirit World and talked to the trees and all things living. They would always give thanks to Mother Earth for her beauty and healing. The humans knew the names of the herbs and plants around them and were familiar with those which could cure different illnesses."

Another troll started to talk excitedly. "Then humans became arrogant and thought they knew best. They thought they were truly wise and had nothing to learn from others with their narrow-minded ideas. They began to doubt the power of the plants and the old ways were laughed at. Money became very important to them and more and more woodlands were cut down so that more and more crops could be grown to feed more and more cattle."

The troll paused to take a breath, but before he could continue, another troll chipped in. "Young children also came to know no better than to sit in front of a strange box pressing keys. For many of them, this has become their real world. And now, the real world of having fun running about in the woods and fields and learning about the wonders of nature is lost to them."

Now, everybody wanted to be heard. Finally a much older troll started to speak. "Slowly, the spirit world and earthly beings like the trolls, elves and gnomes kept away from human contact and so the humans have lost their ability to listen to Mother Earth."

All the trolls began nodding silently in agreement.

"Please, sirs," asked Jack, learning from Ruby's polite manners. "This is all very well, but where do we come in? And who or what is Mondrilla?"

"Whilst all this has been happening to the Earth, the power of Mondrilla has grown. It is a dark, malicious energy. It feeds on fear, greed and negative thoughts. We in the spirit world are losing the strength to fight it. One way is to wake humans to what they are doing before it is too late. They need to respect Mother Earth and realise they are part of this natural world, just like us. If they destroy nature, they will destroy themselves."

The older troll sat down. He was looking exhausted by his efforts and the other trolls were looking at him with some concern.

"The Spirit World has been waiting for you two to help put things right. You have to stop Mondrilla's power before it is too late."

Jack was deep in thought now. He knew they had to take the Wood Betony back for the elves, the Burdock to purify the rivers, and the Elder to protect the woods. With a little bit of luck, he and Ruby could probably do that. But he really wasn't at all sure how the two of them could stop something as powerful as Mondrilla.

Tobin seemed to read his thoughts.

"Just remember Jack, Mondrilla feeds on fear and negative energy. That is how it has grown so powerful in this world. We are here to help you overcome your fears so you can face it."

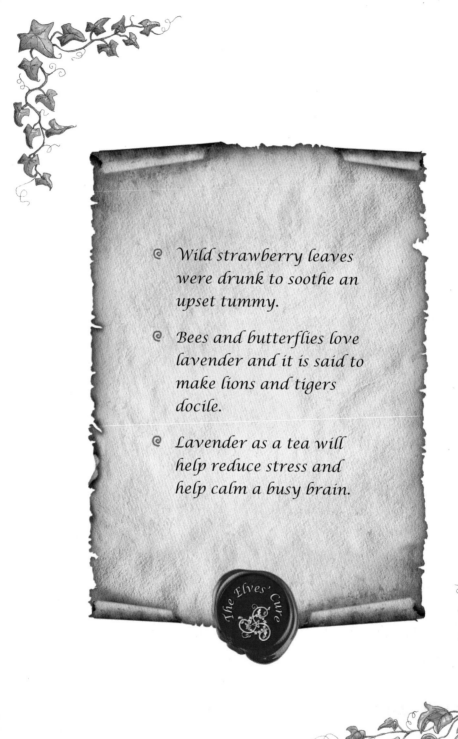

- Wild strawberry leaves were drunk to soothe an upset tummy.

- Bees and butterflies love lavender and it is said to make lions and tigers docile.

- Lavender as a tea will help reduce stress and help calm a busy brain.

The Elves' Cure

Chapter Ten

Facing Their Fears

Ruby and Jack had listened to this long, sad talk. There was nothing they could say. They finished their meal and sat in silence. Both were thinking of the huge responsibility they had been given. Tobin returned, also looking quite sad and took them to the bank of the silver stream.

"It's time for you two to let the stream help you. Be careful as you do so. The stream has the power to wash away all fears. Whatever you are afraid of will confront you in the water. But remember - your fears are all in your mind. You can let them go."

Tobin knew this would be almost as bad as meeting Mondrilla, but it had to be done.

"It will just be like a powerful dress rehearsal."

Now Ruby remembered the Elderflower. "Can I have some Elderflower from your rucksack for protection, Jack?" She bravely put her toe in the water. Immediately, her leg was entwined by a silvery snake. This was a creature she was very, very afraid of. "Oh no! This is truly terrible!" she shouted in what quickly became a high-pitched scream. The snake was tightening its grip and pulling her down but although Jack was yelling at her to hold on, he had no idea what she was screaming at!

"Put your other foot in, Ruby!"

Something made her turn to watch Jack. He was speaking but Ruby could hear no sounds. She tried to lip-read what he was saying. All she could make out were the words "other foot." Without having any real idea why, Ruby put her other foot in the water. At once, the serpent loosened its grip and slithered away.

Poor Ruby was not really up to more challenges, but she ventured to put her right hand in the water and the stream vanished. Instead, she found herself standing on the ledge of a very high cliff. There was barely enough room to put both feet down and under her feet she could feel the rock crumbling! Yet, there was nothing to grasp hold of to steady herself. She could feel herself starting to overbalance. 'Help! I hate heights!" she screamed. Terrified, her whole body shaking now, she remembered the encounter with the snake. Guessing where the stream was, she put her left hand down and felt the silvery water. The image of the high cliff vanished.

Gasping for breath and still trembling from her experience, Ruby climbed out of the stream. "That was truly awful, Jack." She was about to tell her brother what had happened to her but realized that it would make him even more nervous. "I think it's your turn," she said, in the calmest voice she could manage, but she was white-faced and shaking which didn't give him much encouragement!

Jack put his toe in the water and was aware of a many-headed monster coming towards him. Jack found himself wanting to run away but couldn't move his legs. He was stuck fast in the river as the monster moved closer and closer. Although he tried to call out, no sounds came from his mouth. One of the monster's heads eyeballed him! Another head was so close he could feel its foul breath on his face. Then, in a flash, Jack remembered his computer games. The monster looked just like one of the alien creatures. "Phew! I know what this is!" He put his foot deeper in the water as if to challenge the monster and it faded away.

Jack took a deep breath and put his hand in the water. Immediately, he was surrounded by books of all shapes and sizes. The problem was that he was truly terrified of reading! When he looked at the letters on a page, it was as if they were swarms of ants moving around. They all looked jumbled up and confusing. Just when he was beginning to work out a word, the letters would shift around!

Now, to his horror, he saw that he was standing in front of all his classmates. In fact, he was supposed to be reading to the whole school assembly! He could hardly hold the book still because he was

shaking so much. Sweat was running down his face and neck. His hands were so sweaty that the book he held was starting to slip. Jack hadn't told anyone that he found reading so painful, but now there was no escaping his fear.

All of a sudden, Ruby was standing beside him, helping him with the words. She had realised, almost too late, that the warning not to separate applied here too. She had watched Jack put his hand in the water and he had stepped in further and begun sinking. Ruby had jumped in to wake him up and save her brother!

They needed to work together, gaining strength from each other. Jack and Ruby were beginning to realise that the dangers were not as terrifying as they had anticipated. With a little determination fears could be overcome, but the children were exhausted by their efforts and after all, this was only a rehearsal. The real challenge still lay ahead.

- A useful way to calm fearful thoughts is to focus on your breathing. A calm belly breath brings a calm mind.

- Imagine or sit with a tree and share each other's breathing. The tree uses your carbon dioxide from your breath and turns it to oxygen for you to breath. Then, imagine tree roots growing from your feet into the earth and merging with the tree. Hug the tree as a thank you.

- We all have our own fears and they can be alchemised with compassion and light to help remember our inner power, balance, gifts and talents.

The Elves' Cure

Chapter Eleven

Mondrilla the Evil One

As if speaking loudly would summon up the Evil One, Tobin whispered to Jack and Ruby, "I think you two are ready. It's time to meet Mondrilla. Remember, it feeds on fear so make sure you have lots of positive, warm loving thoughts when it comes near. Take a sip of this Borage potion. It will give you the courage you need."

Tobin led them to a vast doorway carved in the rock. He and the other Trolls stepped back. This was a human quest. Jack led the way, brave again and determined to show no fear. It was as if facing his fears in the silver stream had really given him the courage needed to face this monster.

There was a strange screeching noise in the distance and they both instinctively gripped their precious

herbs even tighter. "Keep thinking positive thoughts, Ruby," Jack whispered.

It was becoming increasingly difficult to see their way in the gloomy tunnel and, for some reason, Ruby had taken the lead. In fact, Jack could no longer see her.

Suddenly, she was there facing him. It was his sweet little sister, except something was wrong. Jack stared at her, aware that there was something different about her. Then he realized what it was. Her eyes were a luminous green and seemed to be piercing right through him! His whole body was becoming strangely chilled and he had a sense that all the energy was being sucked out of his body. An inner voice told him to thrust the magical Vervain into Ruby's face.

"I know you are not Ruby," was all he could utter. But that was enough. The image in front of him disappeared as quickly as it had come and now his little sister was running back down the tunnel towards him.

"Jack! Jack! What was that? I was pushed forward but then I couldn't move."

"That was Mondrilla. It is shape-shifting." Jack felt himself growing in confidence as he remembered all he had been told in his dreams. "The Vervain seemed to frighten it but I know it will be back."

Sure enough, they heard the strange screeching further down the tunnel, but found their way blocked by sharp-thorny brambles. Everywhere there were green eyes, getting closer and closer.

"That's Mondrilla, Ruby." Jack was sure now. "Remember, it feeds on fear."

"Yes, and we need to work together. Quick, hold out your magic Vervain! I've got the powerful Elderflower!"

The two children stood unmoving, holding the two powerful herbs in front of them. The green eyes raced closer, swirling around Jack and Ruby in an evil cloud. The stench of rotting flesh was almost unbearable.

Just before it looked as if the eyes would strike both of them, they heard a loud sigh and the eyes were blown away.

"Phew! It's gone again. I think I know what is happening," whispered Jack, as the brambles and eyes disappeared in the distance. "Mondrilla can't keep its shape, even when it's shape-shifting."

"It must be because we have let go of our fears," suggested Ruby, sounding more confident.

"Yes, Ruby, but it's more than that," replied her brother. "These amazing herbs are doing the rest for us."

"Clever children!" Jack and Ruby immediately recognised the voice. It was Georgius, standing in front of them, grinning.

Chapter Twelve

The Golden Casket

"You can't fool me!" screamed Jack. "I know who you are!" Georgius was still grinning at him. His piercing green eyes held his stare. "You just shape-shifted again Mondrilla!"

Ruby stepped back, frightened of what Mondrilla would do next, but suddenly the grin disappeared from Georgius' face and he started to change shape again. This time, however, the shapes continued changing but fading as they did so.

"Look! See!" exclaimed Jack. "We have more power than this horrible creature!"

The gloomy greyness seemed to be clearing. "Look!" cried Ruby. "I can see a bright ray of light, the colour of a rainbow, coming from behind that creature. It's as if it's guarding what's there."

"Clever you," said Jack and he really meant it. "It looks like a box or a casket."

As the couple moved closer, the rainbow rays became more intense. "How beautiful!" exclaimed Ruby.

"This is what I have seen in my dreams!" Jack exclaimed. The images of Mondrilla were completely fading now. "Let's open it."

Ruby wasn't sure. She'd had too many nasty experiences recently, but Jack had now learned to trust his instincts. He cautiously stepped forward and, ever so slowly, lifted the lid of the casket. Magically, the most beautiful magenta -flowered plants grew upwards as they watched!

"Wood Betony, I bet you!" yelled Jack. "This is what the elves told us would bring health back to Mother Earth and all the spirits of the plants."

They carefully pulled up the plants and put them in Jack's rucksack. As they did so, more plants grew in the casket.

"Cool! Now we have enough plants for the whole elven world!"

Ruby and Jack were thinking hard now. "We need to take the casket as well. The plants will die before we get them to the elves if we have to pick them. There must be a way to free the casket from the ground and the grip of Mondrilla's power. In any case, we can't carry all the flowers – they are increasing by the minute!"

"I wonder if the magic herbs might help us. We've seen their magical powers. Why don't we ask for their help again?"

"We haven't got any water or Vervain left, Jack, but why don't we add the Elderflower and Ramsons to the Wood Betony and see what happens?"

They placed all three herbs on the casket, closed their eyes and asked the plants for help. To the children's amazement, the casket practically jumped out of the ground. As it did so, they were aware of a distant wailing and howling. "Mondrilla!" said Jack and Ruby in unison.

"I guess we should have known that the spirits of the plants were there to help us," observed Ruby, as they marched back down the tunnel towards the trolls, carrying their precious casket.

- *It was believed that Betony cured forty-seven specific disorders.*

- *Today Wood Betony is used as a liver herb to detox the body.*

Chapter Thirteen

The Way Home

There was such a noise at the end of the tunnel. All the trolls were dancing and laughing. Tobin came up to greet them with a huge yellow-toothed grin!

"Well done, you two. What a joy it is to see you back here safe and sound in one piece!"

Jack and Ruby were dazed and exhausted from their ordeal and had no words to share. Then Jack remembered, "Oh no, we've forgotten the Burdock!"

"No problem!" replied Tobin, still grinning. "We have plenty. We use it to help clean the rivers and tree roots. It's down by the silver stream. I'll send the younger trolls to get some for you. Mondrilla cannot stop us now."

"Thank you. Now we have to find our way back."
Jack was suddenly overcome with weariness.

The casket of Wood Betony was shining even more
brightly as the trolls carried the weary siblings to
the entrance of the cavern. Here they were greeted
by the hawk flying over their heads, but it flew off
before they could check the direction.

Jack was thinking hard again now. They had used up
the last of their Vervain, Elder and Ramsons and he
had no idea how they would get back! Then they
heard a familiar roaring sound and a noisy flapping of
wings. Dragus the dragon landed in front of them!

"HOW WONDERFUL TO SEE YOU TWO AGAIN!
IT'S TIME TO TAKE A FLIGHT HOME."

"Still shouting, eh?" joked Jack.

"OOPS! SORRY! BEEN ON MY OWN FOR TOO
LONG! Is that better? Now please climb on my
talons and hold tight!"

Jack and Ruby did as they were told. They were
both a little wary of the dragon, even though they

had faced much worse. The trolls bound twine tightly around them and their precious casket.

"OK. WE'RE OFF! Sorry. Let me try that again. OK, we're off."
With a swish of his purple-green tail, Dragus took off into the skies. The children looked down and saw the trolls waving to them.

"Safe journey, dear ones. The earth spirits are with you," the trolls chanted in unison.

The dragon wove his way through the wood, and Jack and Ruby were suddenly aware that as they flew past the trees they burst into full leaf with an array of many vibrant greens and the birds were singing joyfully. Everything was starting to look healthy again.

"Look!" called out Ruby. "The fields we walked past before are now full of beautiful wild flowers."

"Seems like the Wood Betony is doing its magic work already!" added Jack.

"Looks like Mother Nature knew you were coming!" said Dragus, as he gently landed. "I have to leave you now. Follow the path and you will find your way back to the elves."

"Thank you, Dragus," said Ruby, looking around her at the beautiful trees.

"We will be fine from here," said Jack. "I know it."

In fact, they had only walked a short distance when they heard gentle singing all around them. The forest seemed full of elves who now rushed forward to help them carry the casket.

Soon they were back in the magic glade. The old Druid was standing there, surrounded by the elven elders.

"Well done, brave ones. Your courage and determination just show what can be done to restore the natural balance of Mother Earth. We have so much to thank you for. You will always be welcome here. Remember, our world is your world too!"

The Druid placed the casket on the ground and the Wood Betony grew and grew all around them. Some of the young elves now took the precious plants and began planting them under the trees, singing as they did so.

All around them they could feel the most amazing joyful energy. The young elves were busy preparing a feast whilst others were playing pipes and harps. Even the song birds joined in and the whole ancient wood seemed to be alive again.

Ruby and Jack caught a glimpse of crystal-like wings. It was Aqua. She seemed even more joyful than before.

"Here's your Burdock, Aqua." Ruby's smile said it all. She knew that the water sprite would be back cleansing the rivers. In a twinkling flash she was gone.

When it was time, Jack and Ruby were taken to the feast and given so many delicious foods that they had never seen or tasted before. Gradually, their energy returned as the young elves danced around them.

After some time, all the elves grew quiet. The Druid was speaking again.

"We will do our part to make sure the woodlands are healthy again." The Druid was serious again. "But your work is only just beginning. When you start to teach other young humans how they can save Mother Earth, there will be no stopping them." He paused for a moment. "It is your future after all."

Exhausted but happy, Jack and Ruby started on the long walk home. Without warning, Ruby suddenly stopped.

"I've just thought. How are we going to explain to Mum where we have been all this time?"

"We tell her the truth. That we've been saving Mother Earth!" replied Jack.

Silly boy, thought Ruby. "We tell her we've been picking wild flowers. That's sort of the truth as well!"

Silly girl, thought Jack. "And where are the flowers we're supposed to have picked?"

"Oh, you're right! This needs some serious thought," Ruby added.

Jack didn't reply. Meeting Mum could be almost as challenging as meeting Mondrilla, he thought.

The end

Or is it just the beginning?

Sarah Hillyer is a practising herbalist on the south coast of England. She has 30 years' experience as a teacher, culminating as a Head teacher of a school for children with special needs. She then embarked on a new career as a medical herbalist gaining a Bachelor of Science degree. She is deeply rooted in the Celtic traditions and has researched the herbs that were widely used at that time. As with all indigenous cultures, the Earth, plants and trees were respected and revered for their magical and healing properties. The spirit world was not separate.

Sarah is also passionate about environmental issues and is involved as a tutor and volunteer at the Sustainability Centre. This book is very timely as we seek to find ways to reconnect with and protect our Mother Earth. www.southdownsherbalist.co.uk

Patrinia Oolana, is an artist from Hampshire, completing a degree in Art at Portsmouth University in 1997. Her journey into understanding the importance of our individual connection to nature, and each other, rapidly evolved after choosing a life off grid between 2006 and 2014. Scotland became home for a while where she became a Recreational Ranger, and developed a particular interest in the magick of tree, plant and folklore.

Patrinia is deeply involved with the Sustainability Centre and passionate about wellbeing, developing her skills as a Reiki and a meditation teacher. www.nixinnature.co.uk